The Christmas Rush ©

BY CHRISTOPHER NICHOLSON

The Christmas Rush ©

BY CHRISTOPHER NICHOLSON

chris.nicholson.author

Chris.Nicholson.Author

Foreword:

I wrote this book to help children come to terms with the idea of Christmas and that although receiving gifts is great it is also important we remember that Christmas can also bring families together, sharing love, happiness and cheer. Sometimes we become so busy in the rush of Christmas, we forget what really matters, which is simply being together with those you love.

I love Christmas, it's the best time of the year.

I always get what I want and I always jump with jeer.

Receiving presents is all I care about,
ripping open the paper with a scream
and a shout.

Opening a new bike all shiny and new,
playing my videogames is so exciting...it's true.

But if there is one thing I would change, it's how busy things get, it's always the same.

I have to visit grandparents and say "Merry Christmas", but this is never something that is on my wish-list.

What I want is presents not kisses all warm and wet,
times like these I just want to forget.

My parents are always busy, organising stuff, when Christmas comes around we are always in a rush.

When I was younger we always used to play, swinging in the the sunshine, laughing all day.

WAIT! What if I don't beg them for presents and stop shouting for gifts? Then they might not be in a rush and we could all celebrate Christmas in bliss.

How will I tell them how much I care and that I want them and more memories to share?

I will give them a letter with what I want under the tree, and tell them what I really need.

Dear Mum and Dad, I know you are so busy, but I want you to know what I will ask Santa for this Christmas.

I don't want a bike all shiny and green, I don't want computer games that glue me to the screen.

What I really want is you, to spend time together and celebrate, smiling and having fun just like in our family portrait.

MERRY CHRISTMAS

When I gave Mum and Dad the letter their faces were aglow they said "Let's go ice-skating and play in the snow."

This filled me with joy, knowing we would have more time together, experiencing moments we would always treasure.

From that Christmas on we always had fun, playing together under the frosty sun.

I realise now that toys don't make an amazing
Christmas, it's family and love, which will always be
at the top of my wish-list.

The Christmas Rush ©

CHRISTOPHER NICHOLSON

Christmas Maze Game

Help the boy reach his family so he can celebrate Christmas with them.

Christmas Word Search

```
S L H E E M P P J C M
F R A H R L R R H E
M A S R T U E M R M
A M M R Q H S E I O
A E R I T M E H S R
S N R E L V N H T I
M Z G J O Y T I M E
L O V E S O S S A S
T R Z E L H R Z S F
B M A V M S R T S M
```

Memories   Angel   Rush

Presents   Christmas   Together

Family

Joy

Love

Now you write a letter about what you would like for Christmas . Of course, write the presents you would like but also remember the theme of the story about family and love.

_____

_____

_____

_____

_____

_____

_____

_____

_____

_____

_____

_____

_____

_____

_____

_____

_____

_____

_____

_____

_____

_____

_____

_____

_____

_____

Printed in Great Britain
by Amazon

12095665R00016